Mighty Mighty **MONSTERS**

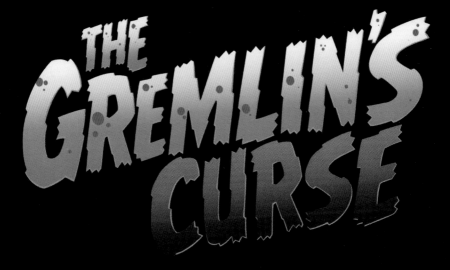

STONE ARCH BOOKS
a capstone imprint

Mighty Mighty Monsters are published by
Stone Arch Books, A Capstone Imprint
1710 Roe Crest Drive
North Mankato, Minnesota 56003
www.capstonepub.com

Cataloging-in-Publication Data is available
at the Library of Congress website.

ISBN: 978-1-4342-3894-8 (library binding)
ISBN: 978-1-4342-4228-0 (paperback)
ISBN: 978-1-4342-4651-6 (eBook)

Summary: Vlad the usually unflappable
vampire is having a really bad day -- so bad
that he begins to wonder if he's cursed!
The Mighty, Mighty Monsters try to help
him out, but they seem to only add to
Vlad's bad luck. But when the gang spots
a new gremlin following Vlad around, they
begin to wonder if the little imp has cast
a bad luck curse on their friend.

Printed in the United States of America in
North Mankato, Minnesota.
032013
007223CGF13

Mighty Mighty MONSTERS

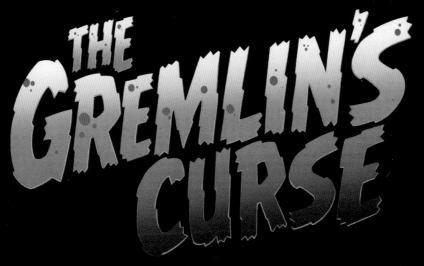

THE GREMLIN'S CURSE

created by
Sean O'Reilly

illustrated by
Arcana Studio

To take on terrifying teachers and homework horrors, they formed the most fearsome friendship on Earth . . .

Mighty Mighty MONSTERS

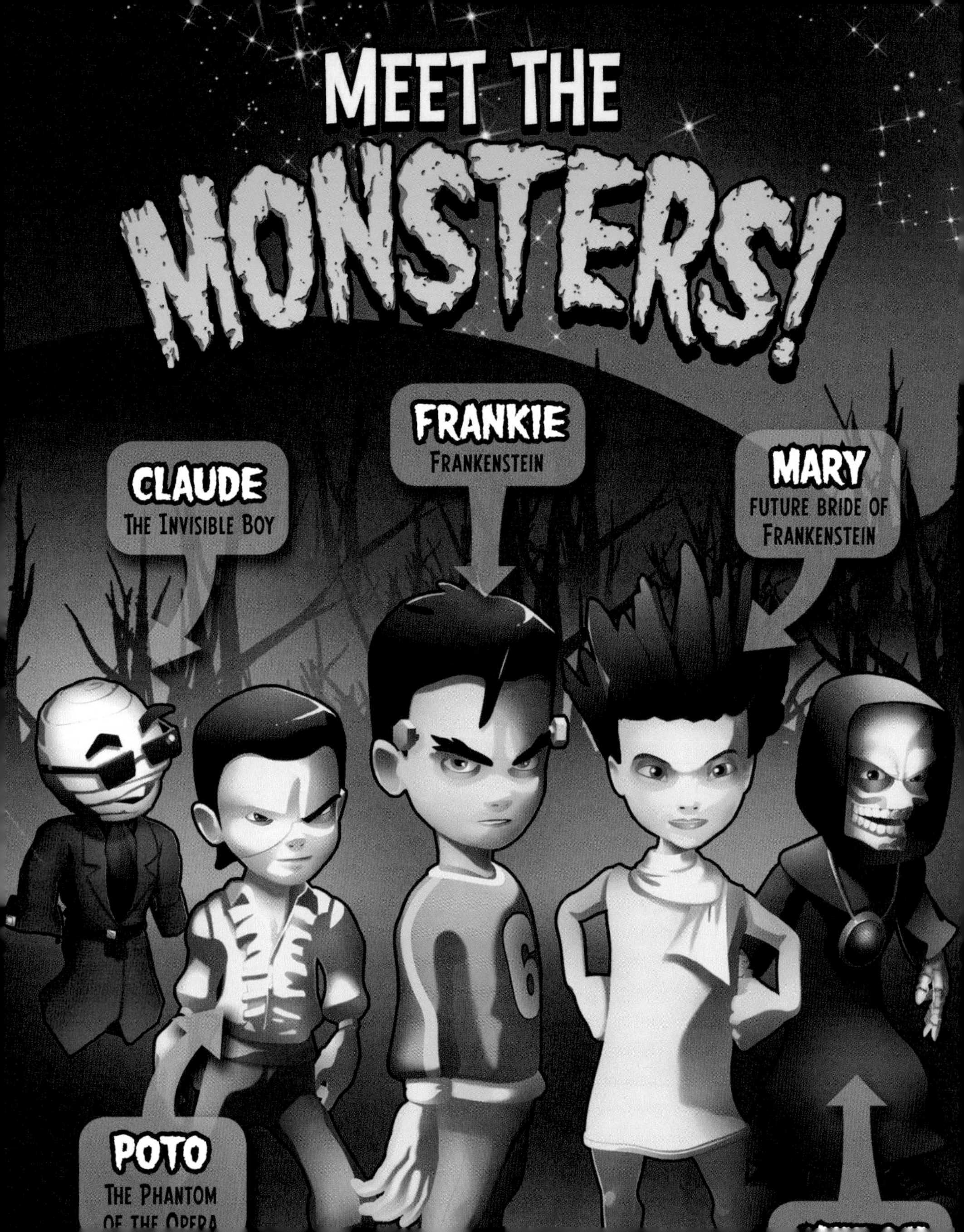
MEET THE MONSTERS!
FRANKIE
FRANKENSTEIN
CLAUDE
THE INVISIBLE BOY
MARY
FUTURE BRIDE OF FRANKENSTEIN
POTO
THE PHANTOM OF THE OPERA

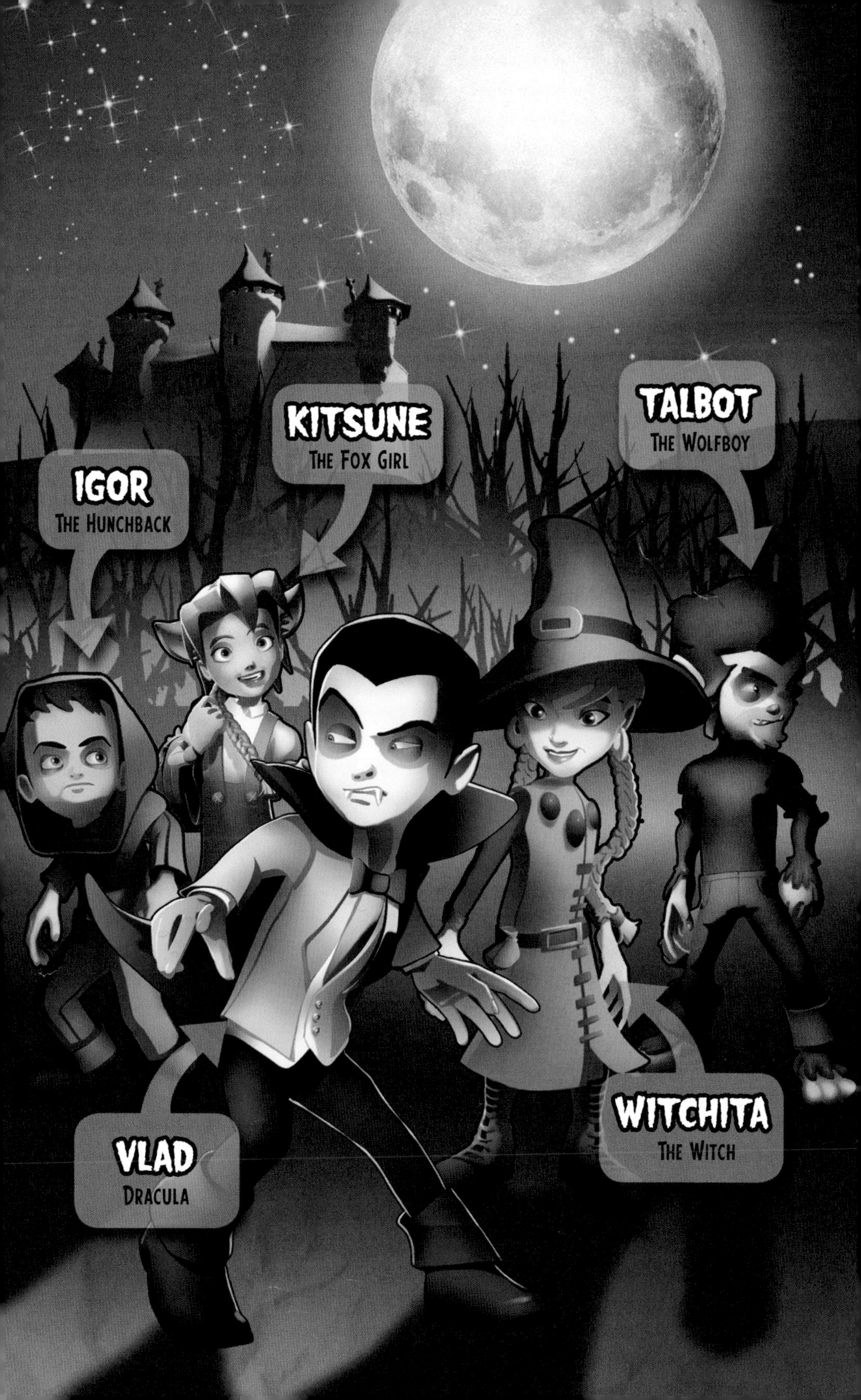
KITSUNE
THE FOX GIRL
TALBOT
THE WOLFBOY
IGOR
THE HUNCHBACK
VLAD
DRACULA
WITCHITA
THE WITCH

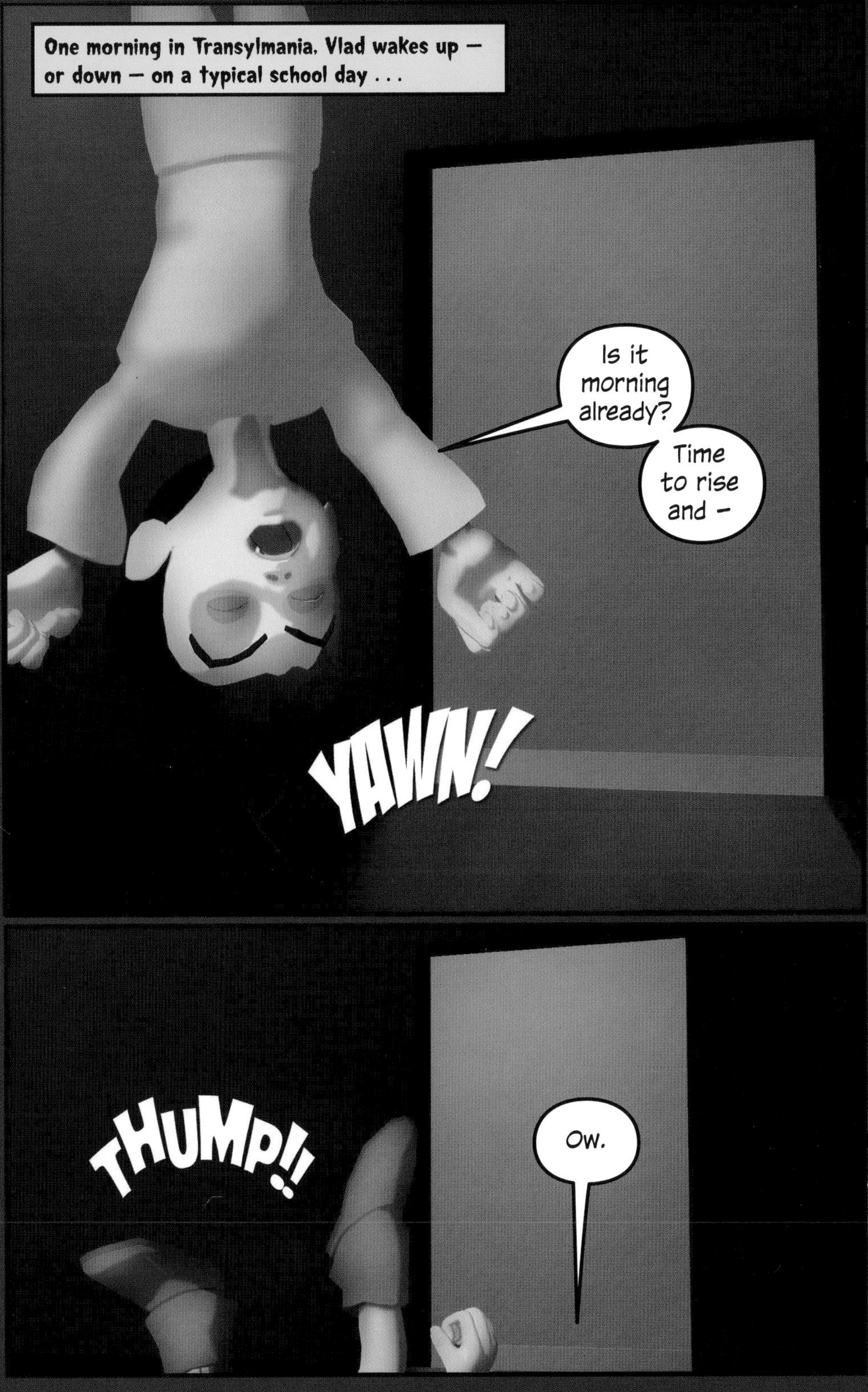
One morning in Transylmania, Vlad wakes up — or down — on a typical school day . . .
Is it morning already?
Time to rise and –
YAWN!
THUMP!!
Ow.

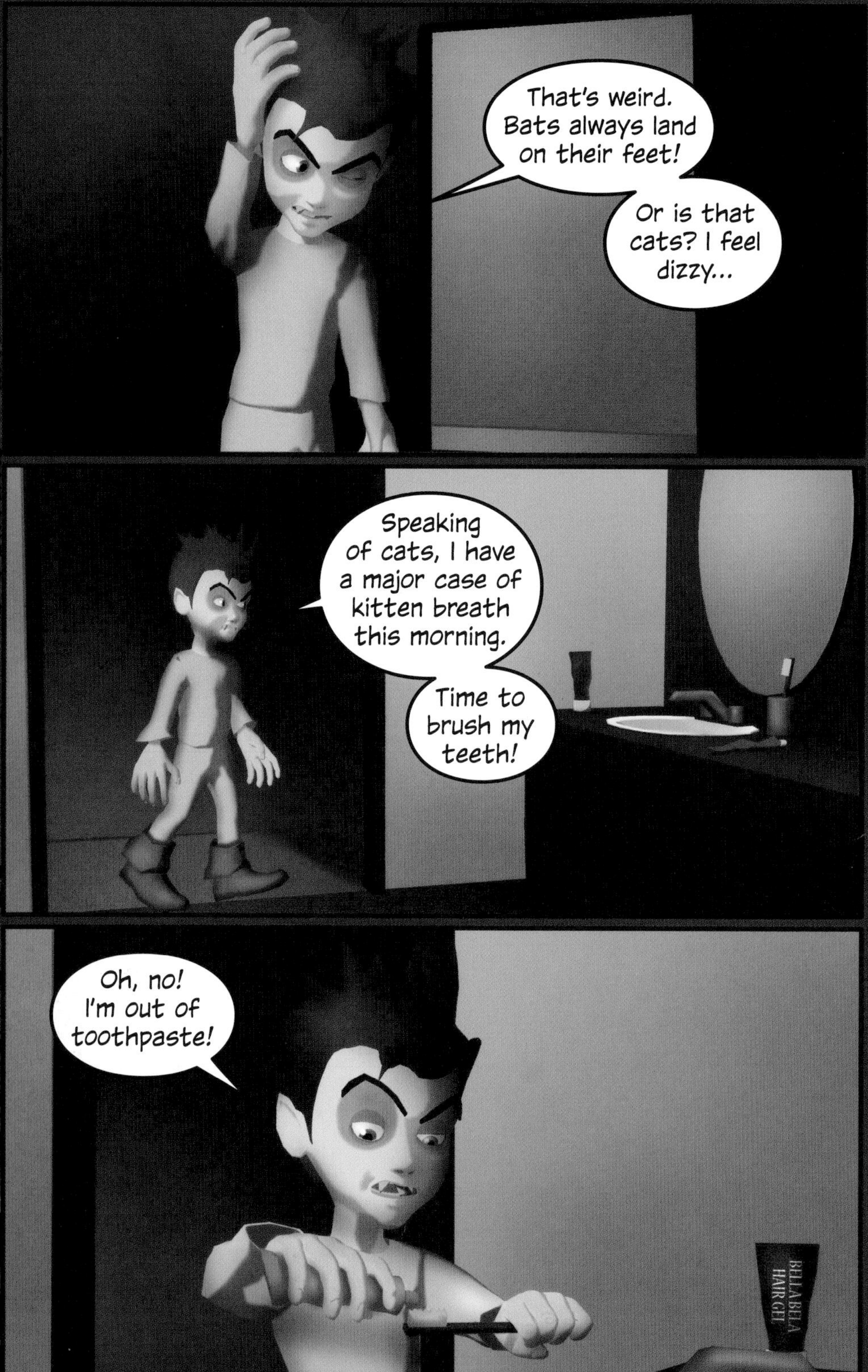
That's weird. Bats always land on their feet!
Or is that cats? I feel dizzy...
Speaking of cats, I have a major case of kitten breath this morning.
Time to brush my teeth!
Oh, no! I'm out of toothpaste!
BELLABELA HAIR GEL

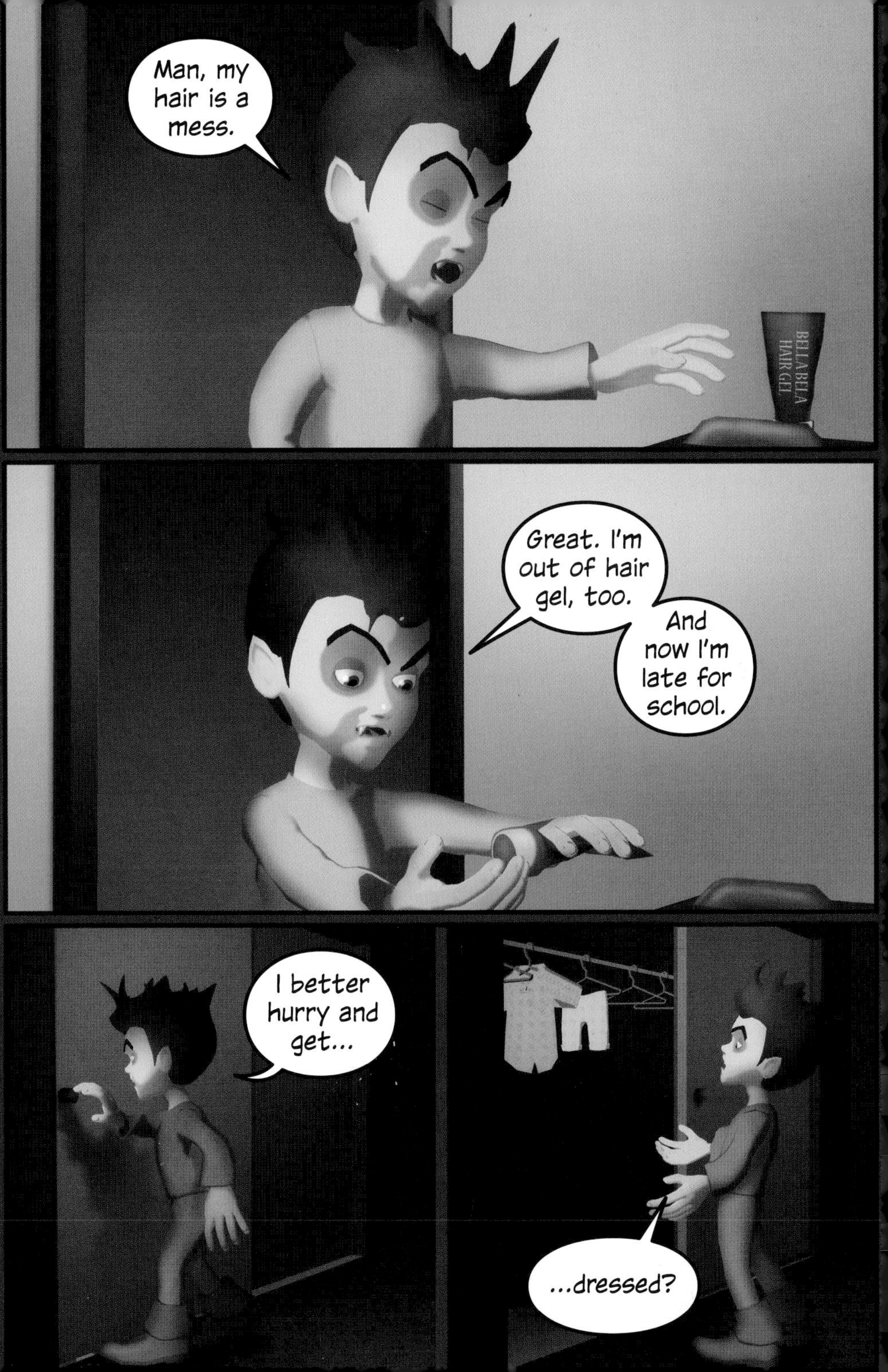

Man, my hair is a mess.
BELLA BELLA HAIR GEL
Great. I'm out of hair gel, too.
And now I'm late for school.
I better hurry and get...
...dressed?

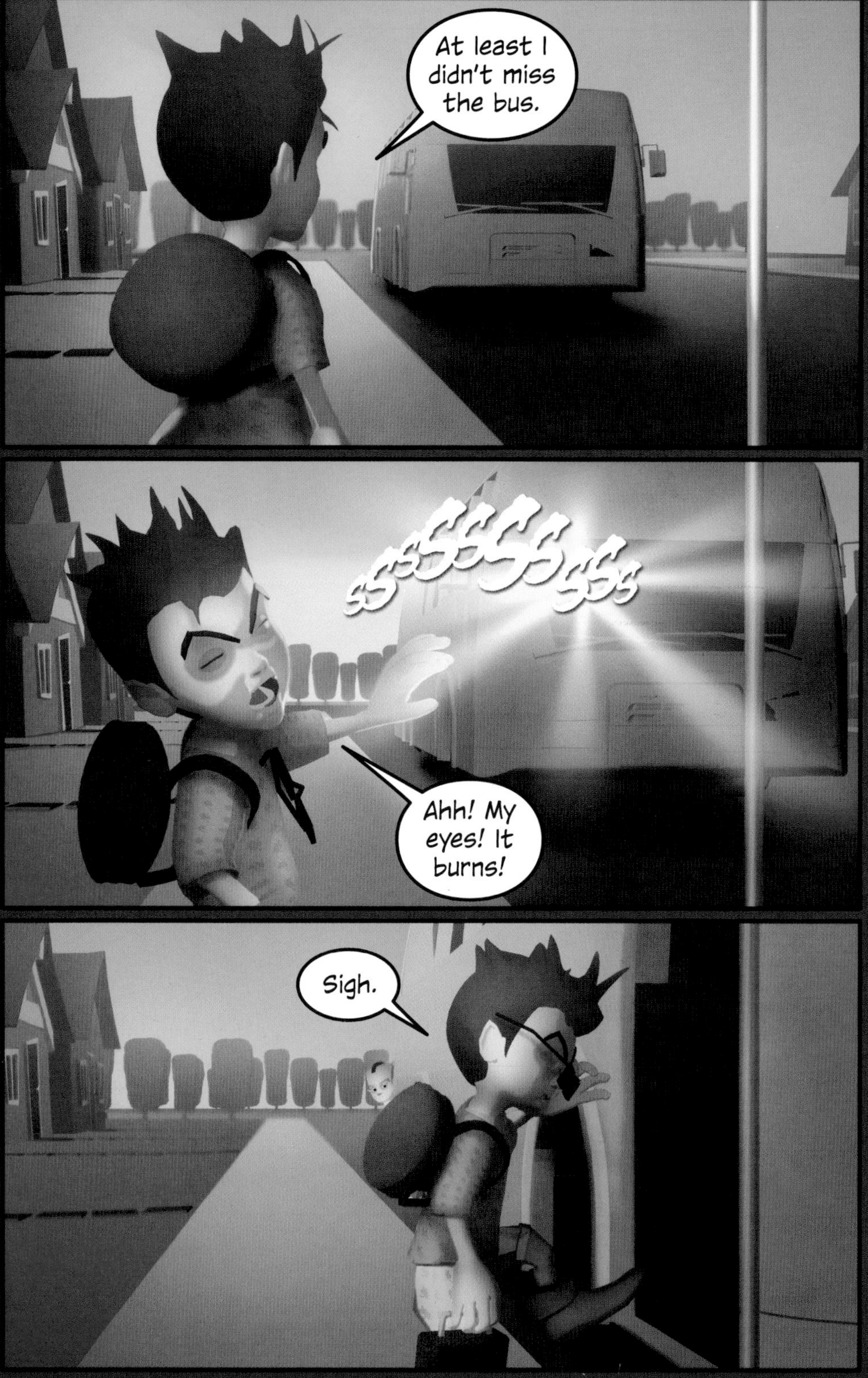
At least I didn't miss the bus.
sSsSSSSSsSs
Ahh! My eyes! It burns!
Sigh.

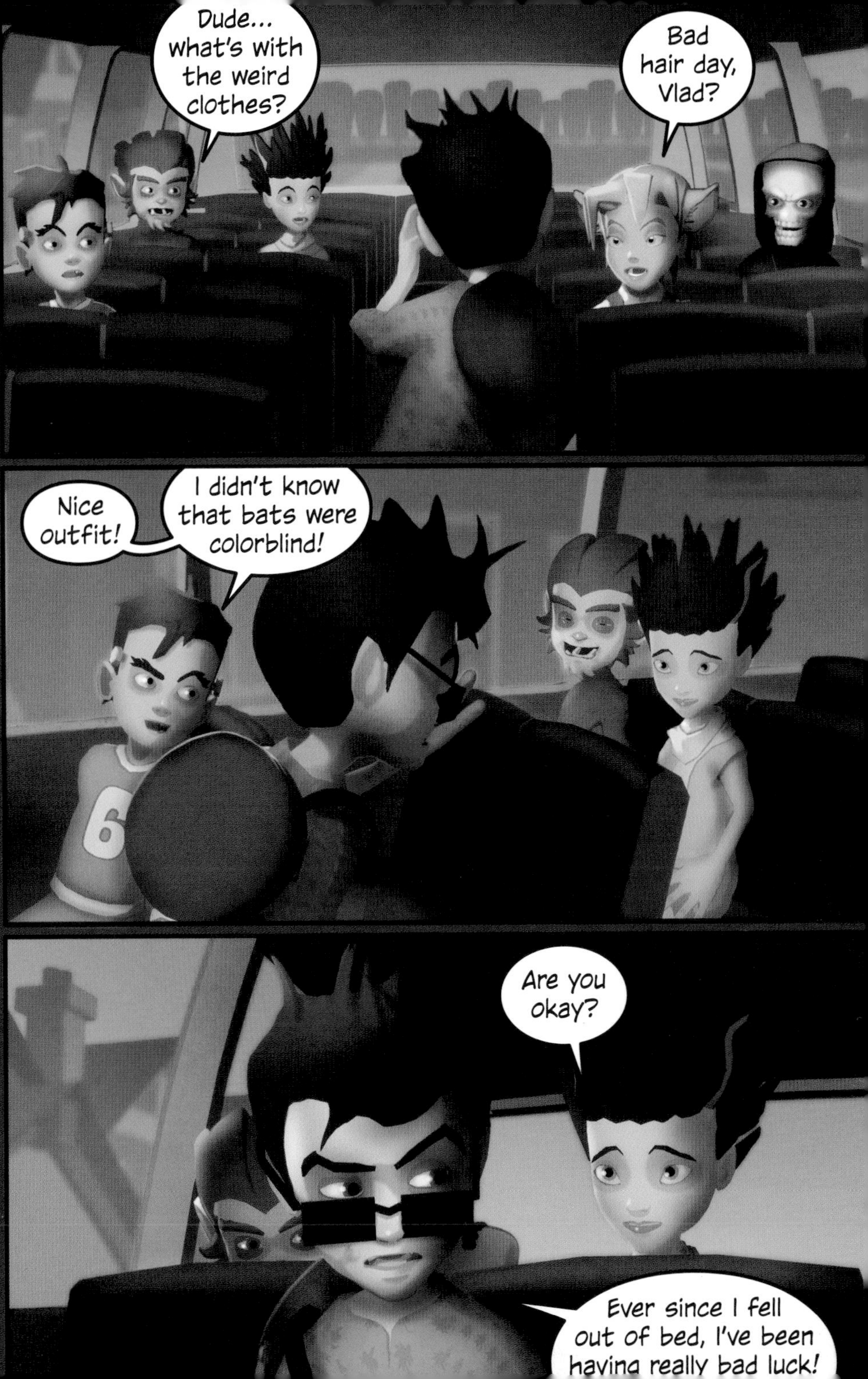
Dude... what's with the weird clothes?
Bad hair day, Vlad?
Nice outfit!
I didn't know that bats were colorblind!
Are you okay?
Ever since I fell out of bed, I've been having really bad luck!

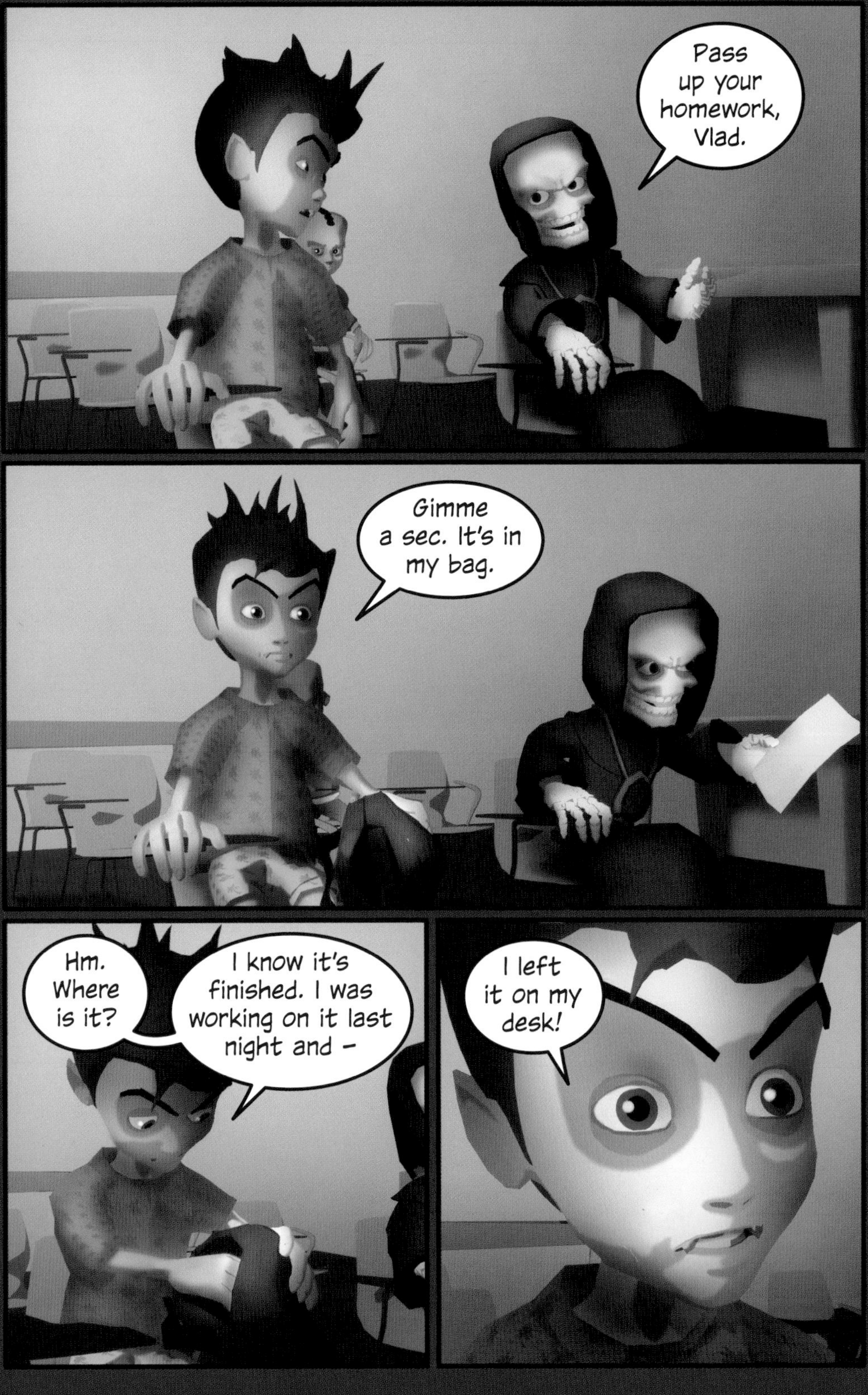

Pass up your homework, Vlad.
Gimme a sec. It's in my bag.
Hm. Where is it?
I know it's finished. I was working on it last night and –
I left it on my desk!

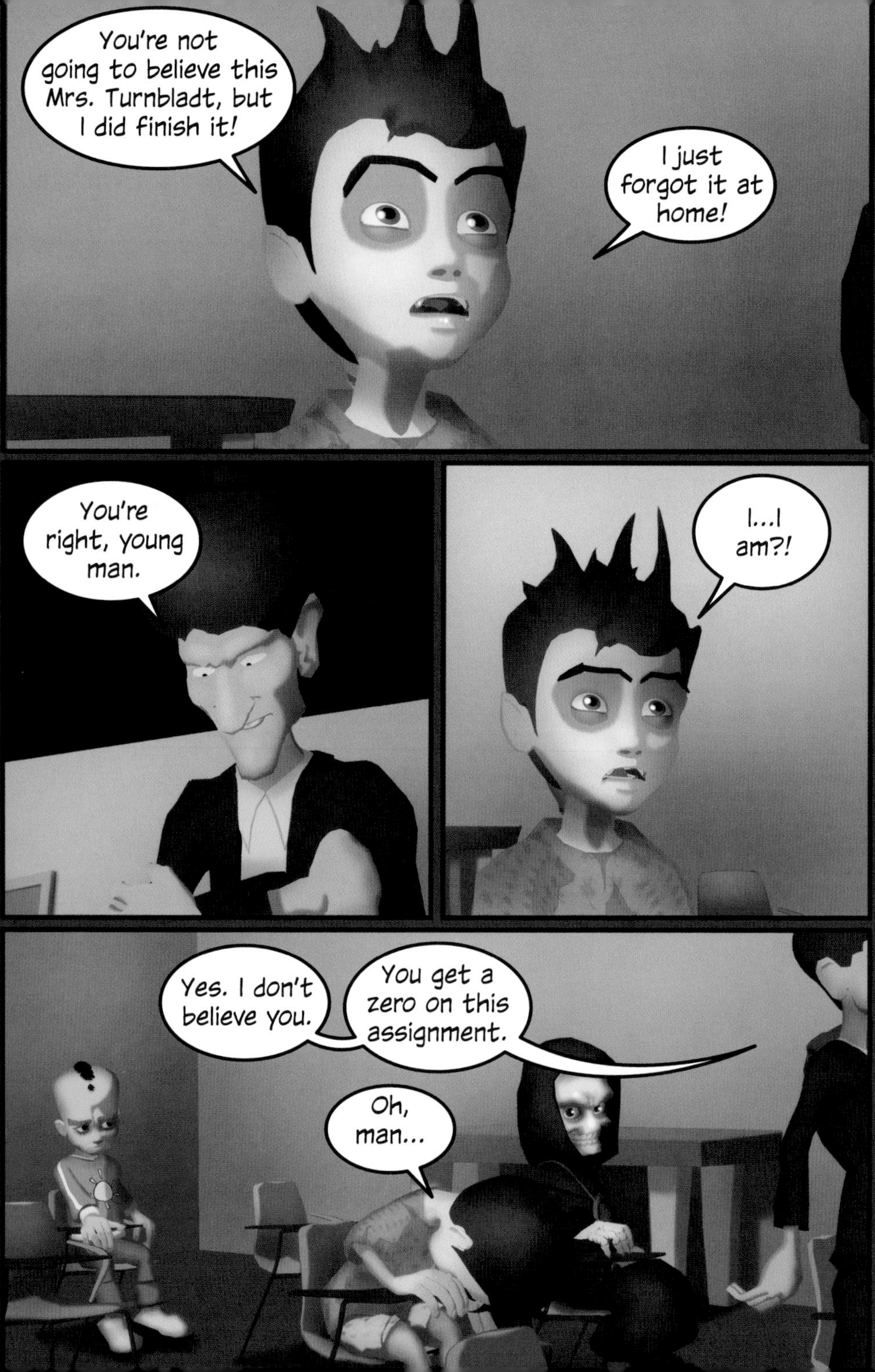
You're not going to believe this Mrs. Turnbladt, but I did finish it!
I just forgot it at home!
You're right, young man.
I...I am?!
Yes. I don't believe you.
You get a zero on this assignment.
Oh, man...

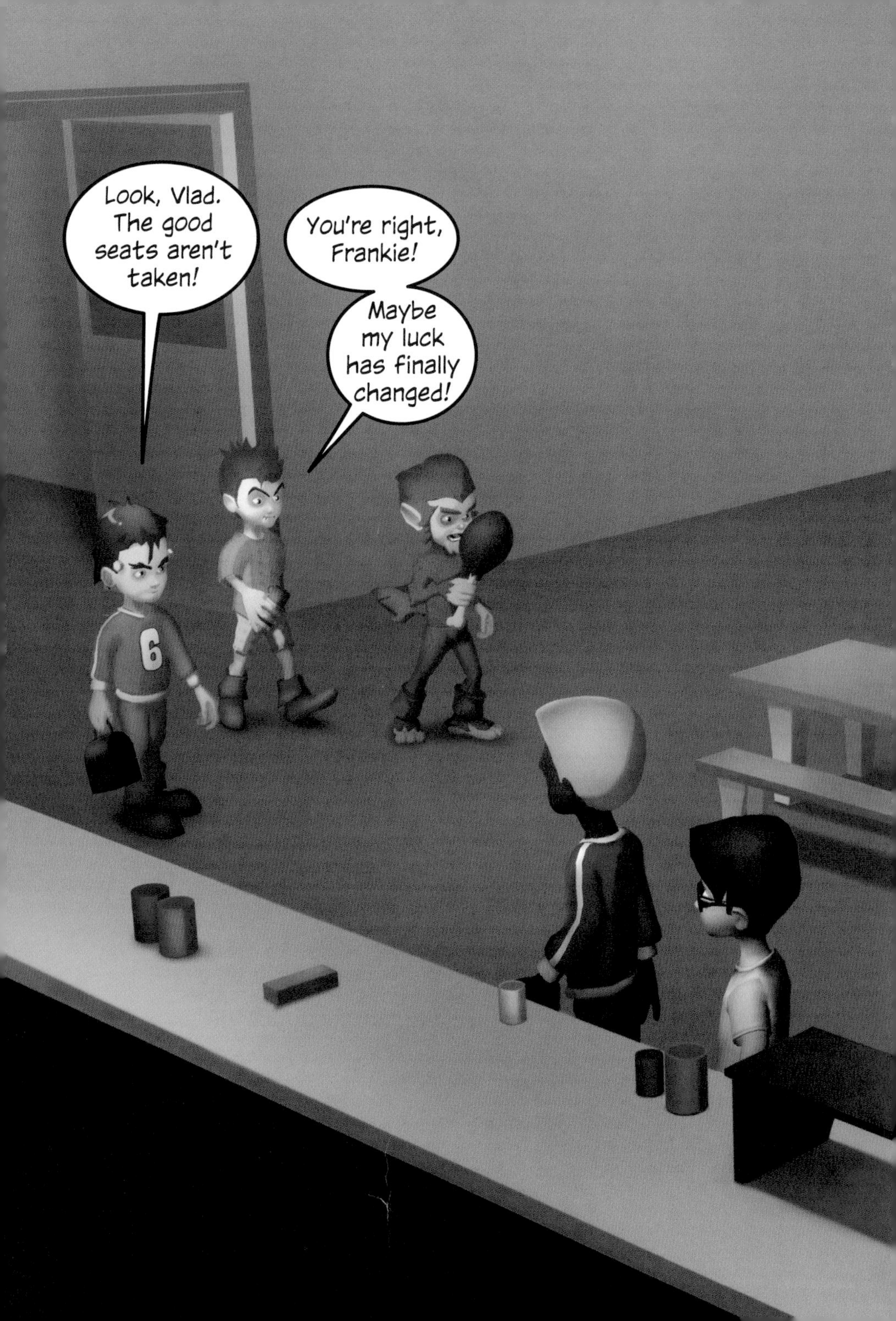
Look, Vlad. The good seats aren't taken!
You're right, Frankie!
Maybe my luck has finally changed!
6

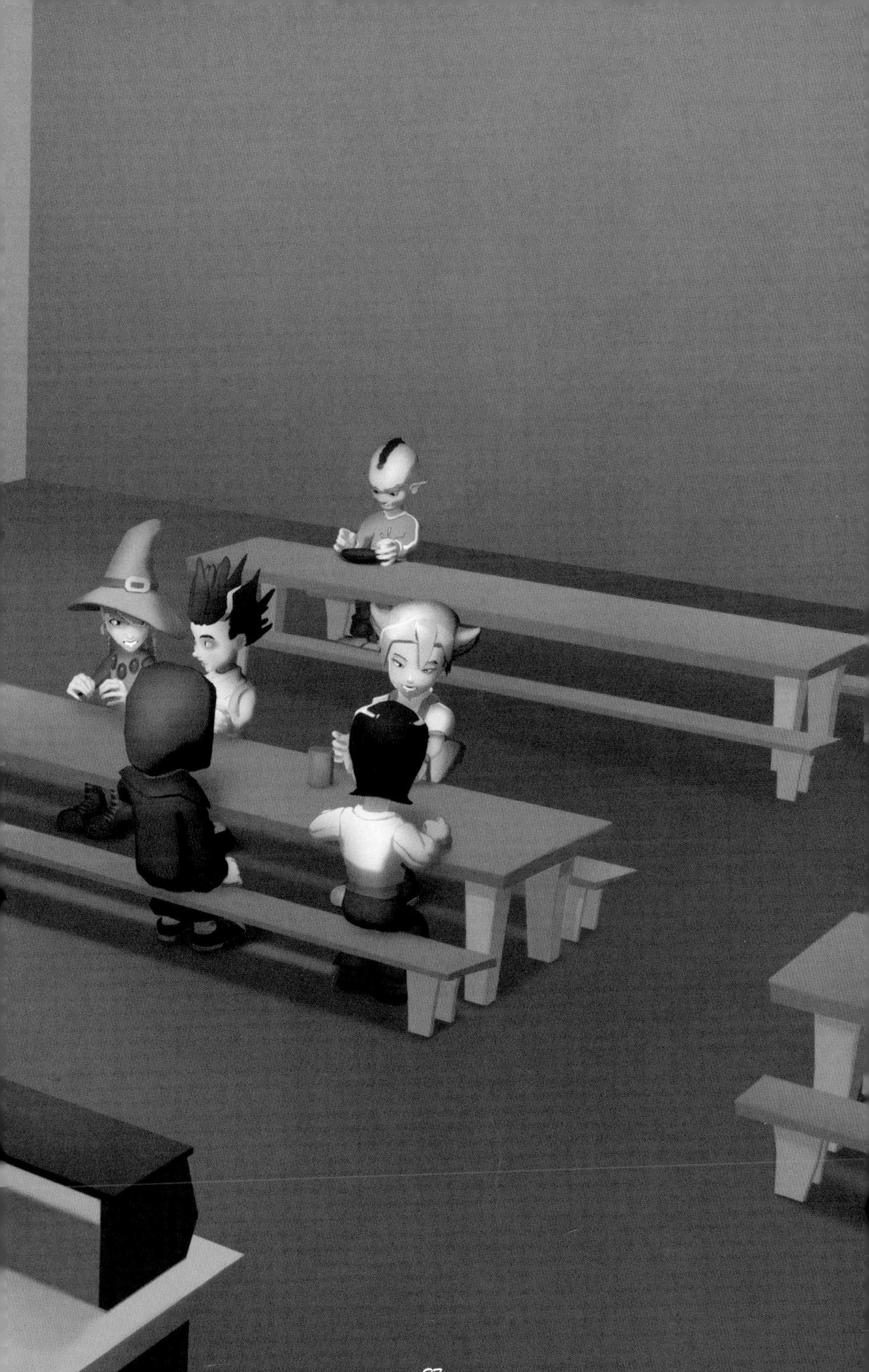

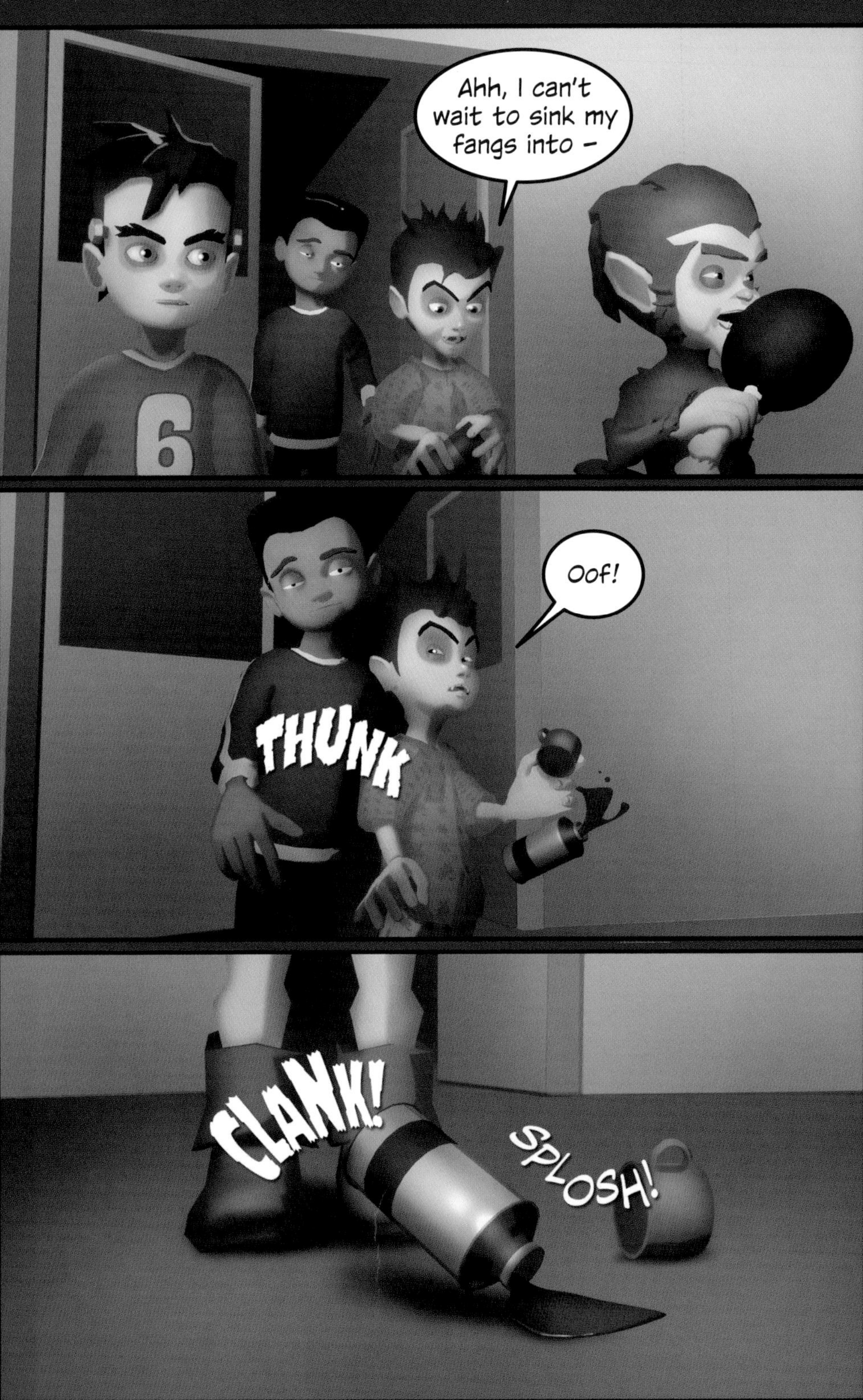
Ahh, I can't wait to sink my fangs into –
6
Oof!
THUNK
CLANK!
SPLOSH!

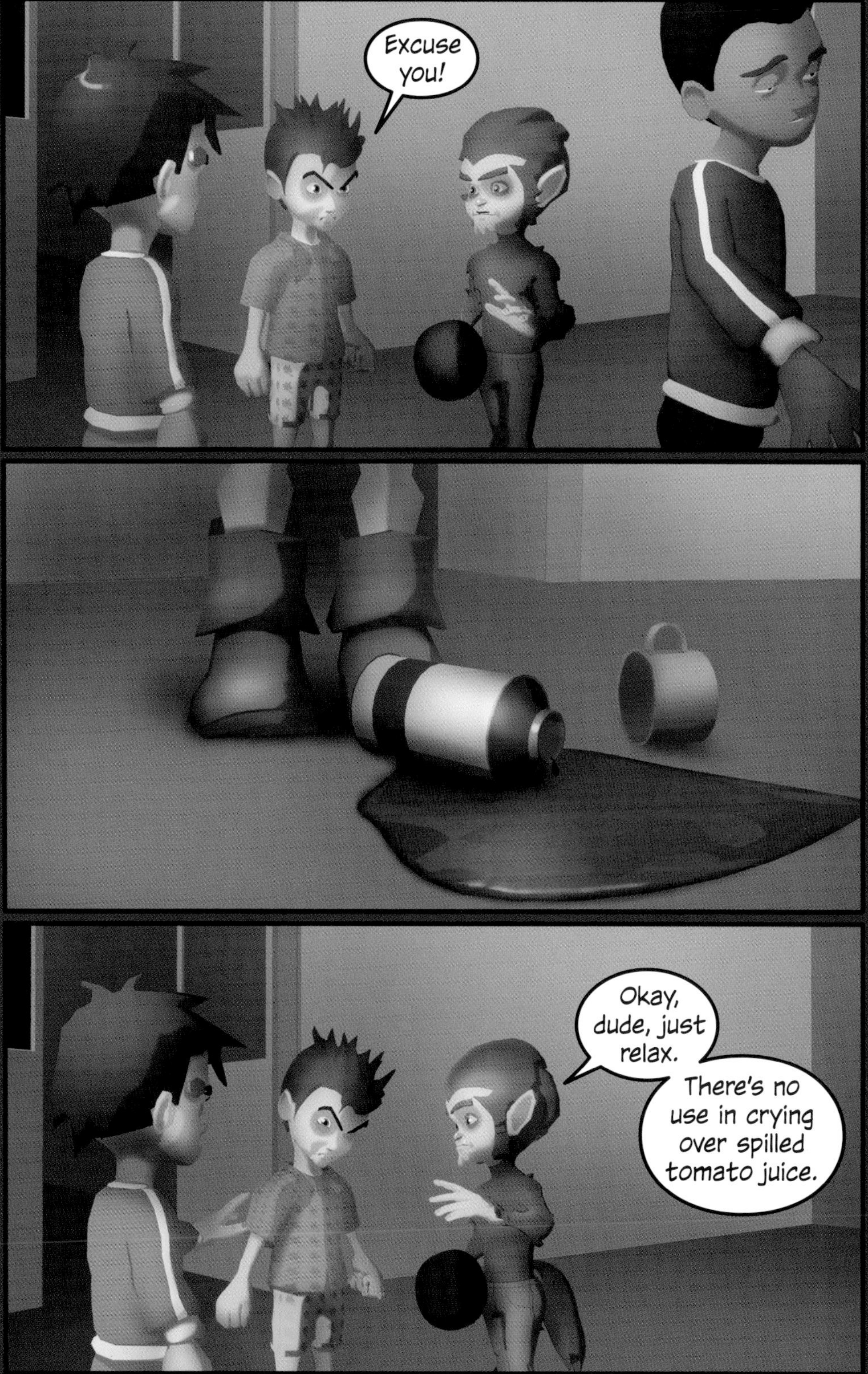
Excuse you!
Okay, dude, just relax.
There's no use in crying over spilled tomato juice.

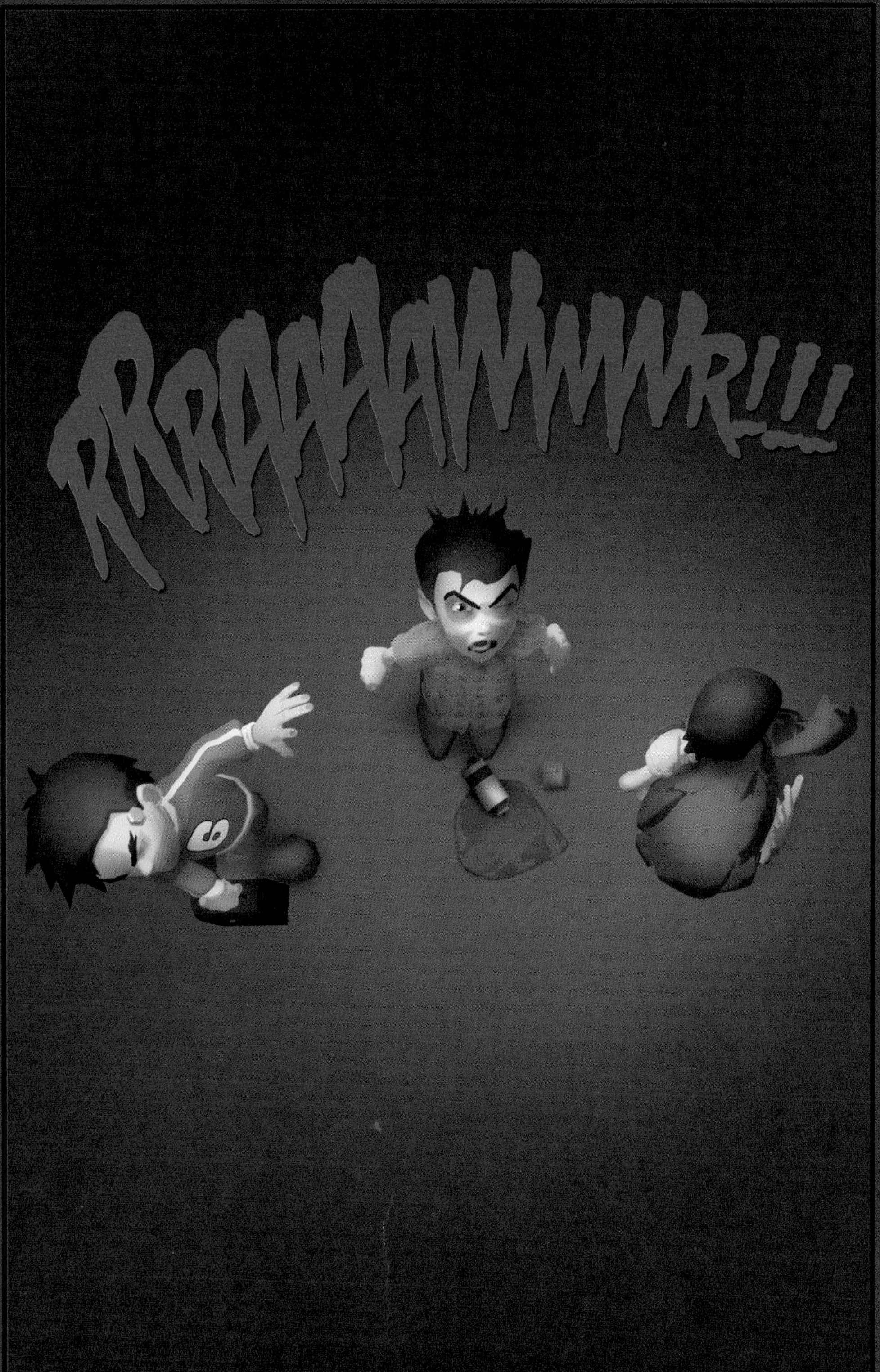
RRROOOAAWWWWR!!!

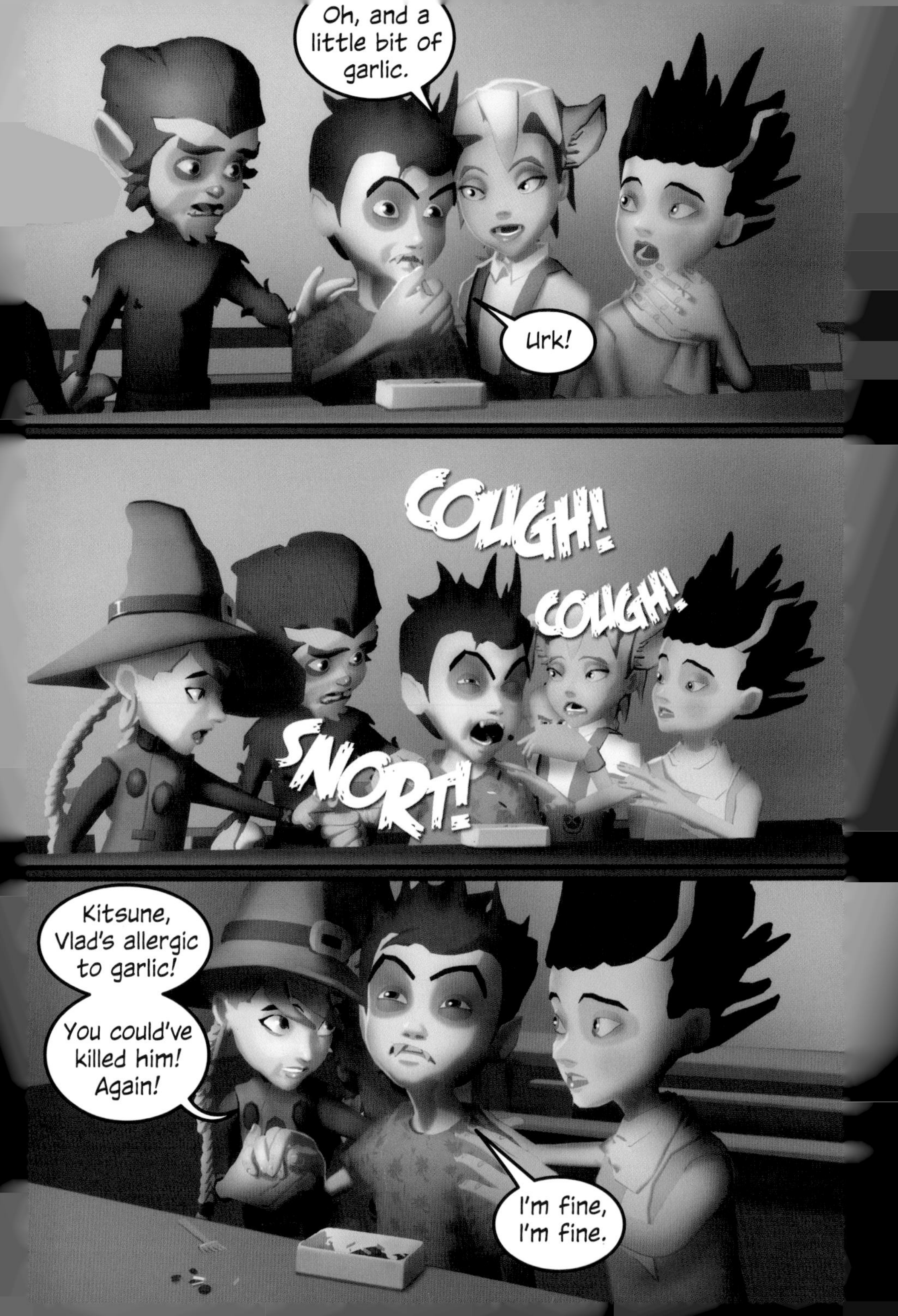
Oh, and a little bit of garlic.
Urk!
COUGH!
COUGH!
SNORT!
Kitsune, Vlad's allergic to garlic!
You could've killed him! Again!
I'm fine, I'm fine.

Suddenly . . .
I think I'm to blame for all this.
I'm really sorry.
Huh? Who are you?
My name's Alexander. I'm new here.

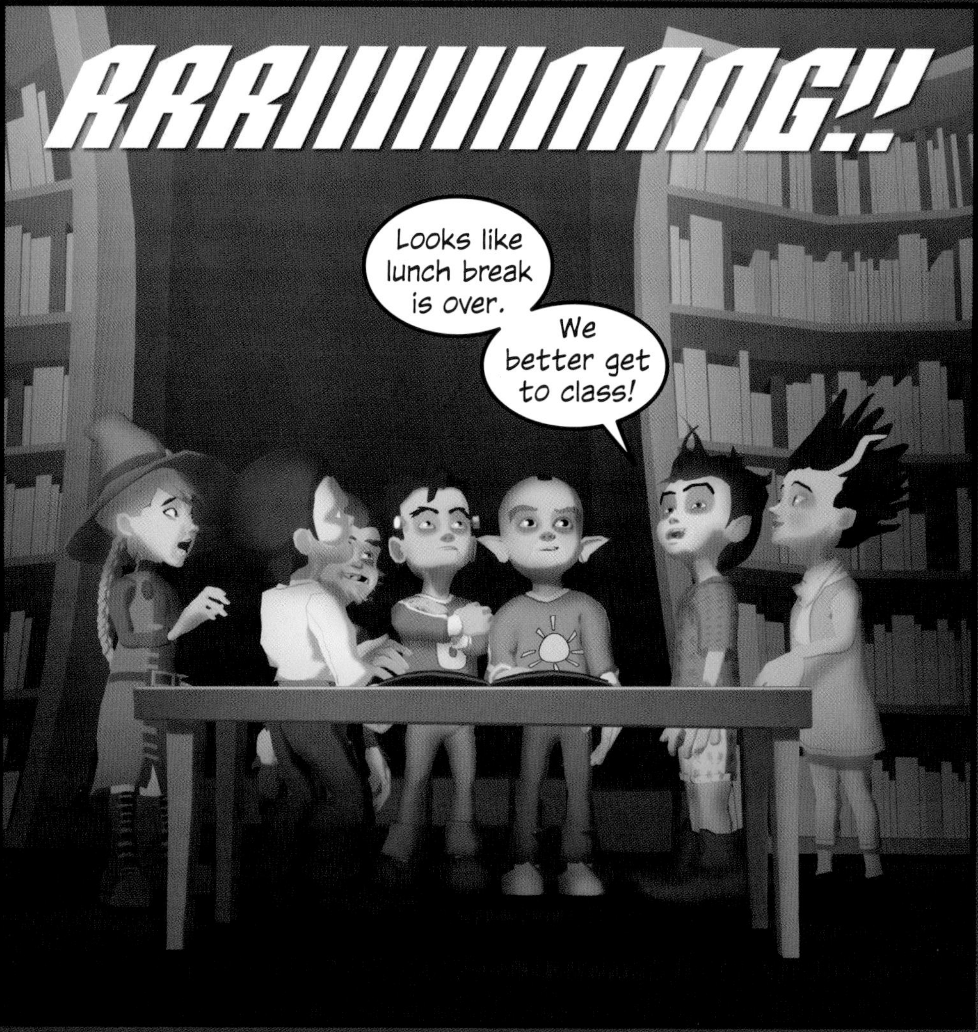
RRRIIIIINNNG!!
Looks like lunch break is over.
We better get to class!

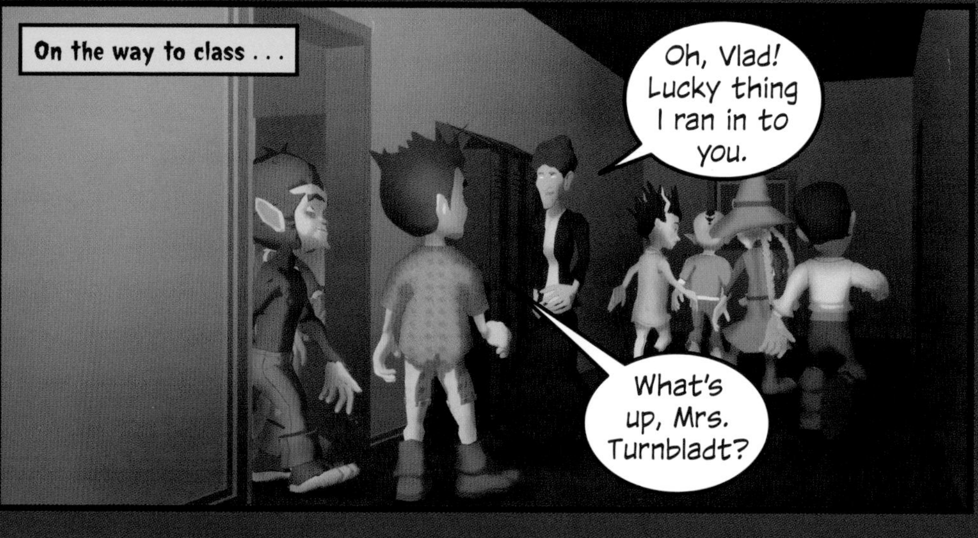
On the way to class . . .
Oh, Vlad! Lucky thing I ran in to you.
What's up, Mrs. Turnbladt?

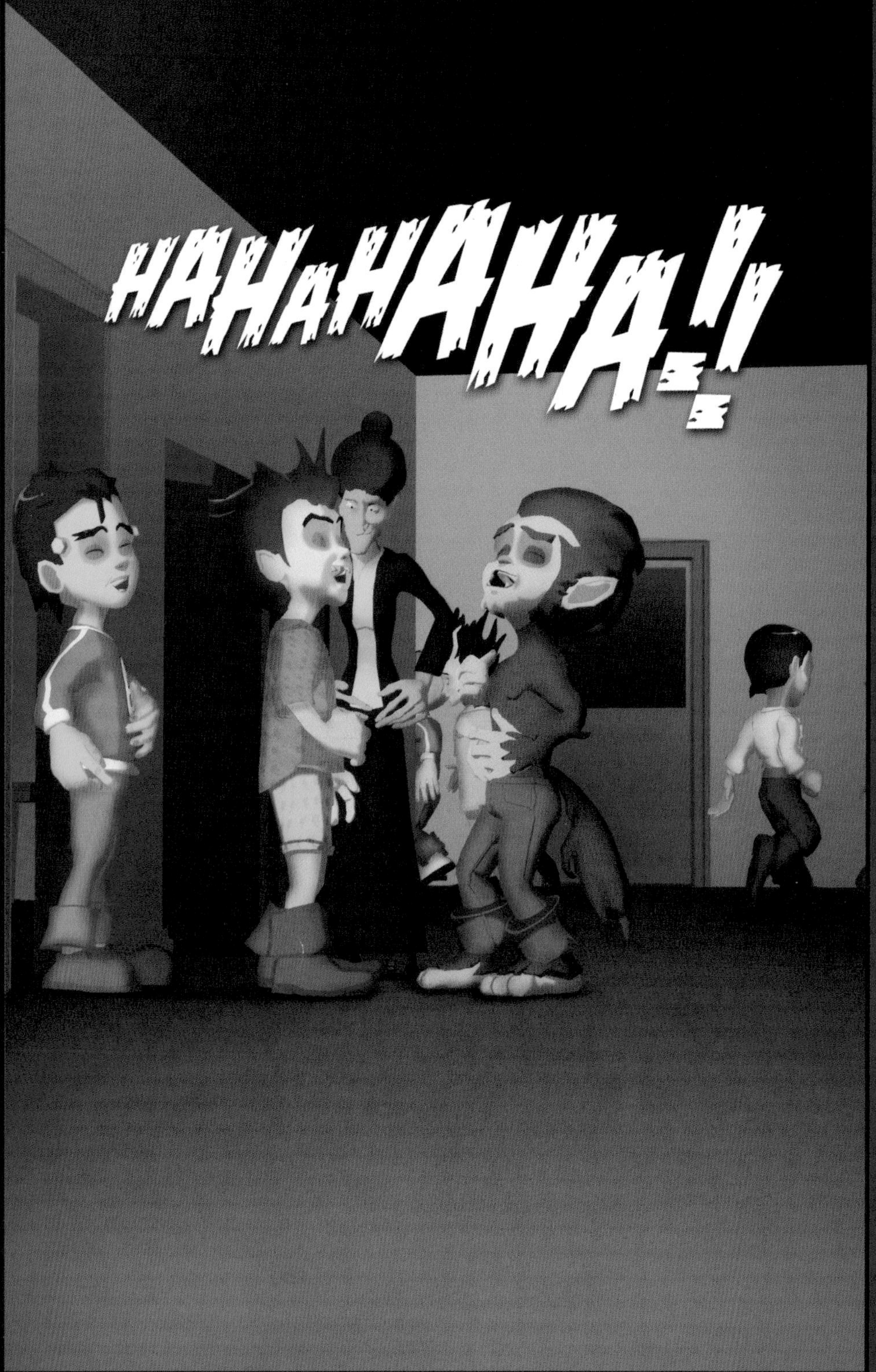
HAHAHAHAHAHA!!

ABOUT
SEAN O'REILLY
AND ARCANA STUDIO

As a lifelong comics fan, Sean O'Reilly dreamed of becoming a comic book creator. In 2004, he realized that dream by creating Arcana Studio. In one short year, O'Reilly took his studio from a one-person operation in his basement to an award-winning comic book publisher with more than 150 graphic novels produced for Harper Collins, Simon & Schuster, Random House, Scholastic, and others.

Within a year, the company won many awards including the Shuster Award for Outstanding Publisher and the Moonbeam Award for top children's graphic novel. O'Reilly also won the Top 40 Under 40 award from the city of Vancouver and authored The Clockwork Girl for Top Graphic Novel at Book Expo America in 2009. Currently, O'Reilly is one of the most prolific independent comic book writers in Canada. While showing no signs of slowing down in comics, he now writes screenplays and adapts his creations for the big screen.

GLOSSARY

aced (AYSSD)—got a perfect score

breed (BREED)—a particular type of animal

colorblind (KUHL-ur-blined)—if you are colorblind, you cannot see certain colors

curse (KURSS)—an evil spell

electrocuted (i-LEK-truh-kyoo-tid)—injured or killed by a severe electric shock

gremlin (GREM-lin)—a mischievous being that causes troubles for others

knack (NAK)—an ability to do something difficult or tricky

relax (ri-LAKS)—become less tense and anxious

typical (TIP-uh-kuhl)—normal, or in a usual way

undead (un-DED)—no longer alive, but instead animated by a supernatural force, like a vampire or zombie

vegetarian (vej-uh-TARE-ee-uhn)—someone who eats only plants

DISCUSSION QUESTIONS

1. Do you believe in good luck? How about bad luck? Why or why not?

2. Poto brings the other monsters to the library to find information about gremlins. When you go to the library, what do you look for? What are your favorite books? Talk about it.

3. Alexander struggles to find friends as the new kid in school. Have you ever been the new kid at school? What do you think it's like to not know anyone at your school? Talk about the challenges of being a new kid.

WRITING PROMPTS

1. Alexander the gremlin has trouble making friends. How many friends do you have? Do you wish you had more friends? Write about friendship.

2. Vlad has a bad hair day and has to wear mismatched clothing to school. What are some other embarrassing things that could happen to someone at school? Write about a student's really bad school day.

3. Ms. Turnbladt punishes Vlad for forgetting to bring his homework to school. Have you ever been punished for something in school? What happened? Write about it.

Mighty Mighty MONSTERS ADVENTURES

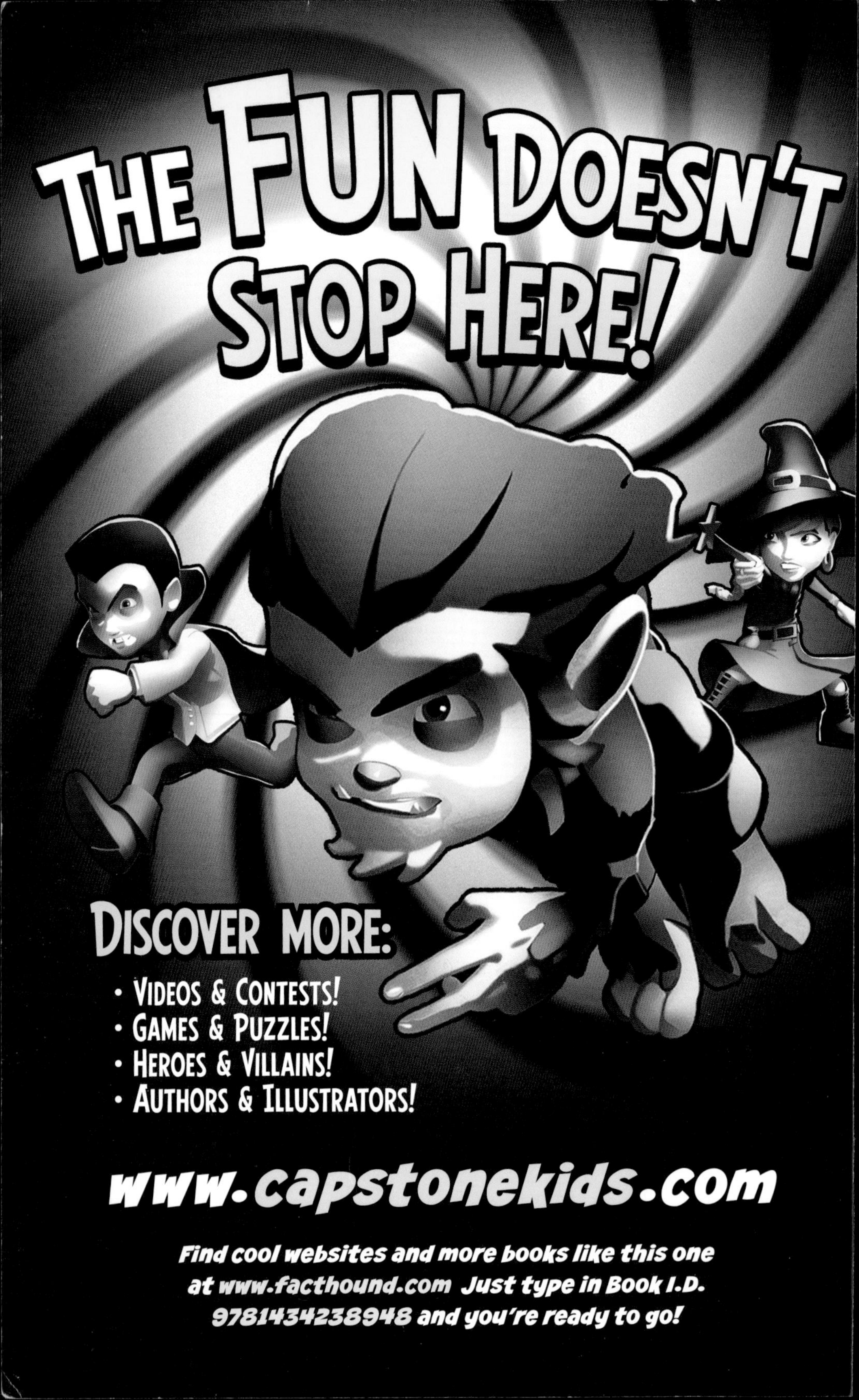
THE FUN DOESN'T STOP HERE!
DISCOVER MORE:
• VIDEOS & CONTESTS!
• GAMES & PUZZLES!
• HEROES & VILLAINS!
• AUTHORS & ILLUSTRATORS!
www.capstonekids.com
Find cool websites and more books like this one at www.facthound.com Just type in Book I.D. 9781434238948 and you're ready to go!